★ BOOK 4 ★
in the **Classroom 13 Series**

THE SUPER ~~Super~~ Awful SUPERHEROES OF CLASSROOM 13

By **Honest Lee** & **Matthew J. Gilbert**
Art by **Joelle Dreidemy**

LITTLE, BROWN AND COMPANY
New York • Boston

Copyright © 2018 by Hachette Book Group
CLASSROOM 13 is a trademark of Hachette Book Group, Inc.
Cover and interior art by Joelle Dreidemy.
Cover design by Véronique Lefèvre Sweet.
Cover copyright © 2018 by Hachette Book Group, Inc.

Little, Brown and Company
Hachette Book Group
1290 Avenue of the Americas, New York, NY 10104

Visit us at LBYR.com

First Edition: March 2018

Little, Brown and Company is a division of Hachette Book Group, Inc.
The Little, Brown name and logo are trademarks of Hachette Book Group, Inc.

The publisher is not responsible for websites (or their content) that are not owned by the publisher.

Library of Congress Cataloging-in-Publication Data
Names: Lee, Honest, author. | Gilbert, Matthew J., author. | Dreidemy, Joelle, illustrator.
Title: The super awful superheroes of Classroom 13 / by Honest Lee & Matthew J. Gilbert ; art by Joelle Dreidemy.
Description: First edition. | New York : Little, Brown and Company, 2018. | Series: Classroom 13 ; book 4 | Summary: After being struck by purple lightning, Ms. Linda and her students gain superpowers and in an effort to save the world, they nearly destroy it.
Identifiers: LCCN 2017011806| ISBN 9780316501095 (hardcover) | ISBN 9780316501125 (paperback) | ISBN 9780316501101 (ebook) | ISBN 9780316501088 (library ebook edition)
Subjects: | CYAC: Superheroes—Fiction. | Ability—Fiction. | Schools—Fiction. | Humorous stories. | BISAC: JUVENILE FICTION / Humorous Stories. | JUVENILE FICTION / Action & Adventure / General. | JUVENILE FICTION / Readers / Chapter Books. | JUVENILE FICTION / Social Issues / Friendship. | JUVENILE FICTION / Readers / Intermediate. | JUVENILE FICTION / Fantasy & Magic.
Classification: LCC PZ7.1.L415 Su 2018 | DDC [Fic]—dc23
LC record available at https://lccn.loc.gov/2017011806

ISBNs: 978-0-316-50109-5 (hardcover), 978-0-316-50112-5 (paperback), 978-0-316-50110-1 (ebook)

Printed in the United States of America

LSC-C

10 9 8 7 6 5 4 3 2 1

 CONTENTS

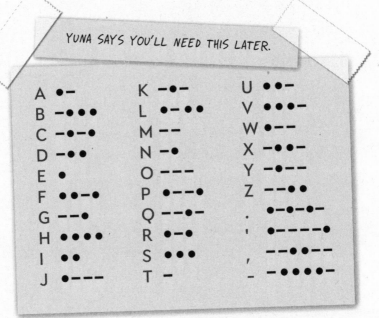

CHAPTER 1
Not-So-Super Ms. Linda

When unlucky schoolteacher Ms. Linda LaCrosse woke up Thursday morning, she hoped it would be another beautiful day. You see, in recent days the weather had been perfect—sunny skies with a crisp, cool breeze.

But not today.

Ms. Linda opened her curtains to see a terrible thundercloud rolling over the neighborhood.

The cloud was black and red, and crackled with purple electricity.

Mumbling and grumbling to herself, Ms. Linda got ready for the day. She put lipstick around her eyes and mascara on her lips. She put a necklace in her hair and a bow around her neck. Then she put her skirt on top and a sweater on the bottom. As she left the house, she whispered, "I feel as though I'm missing something. . . . Oh, yes, my umbrella!"

Ms. Linda then realized she had also left her *keys* inside the house. "I'm locked out of my own home—again," she said to herself. You might be thinking to yourself, *That Ms. Linda sure is forgetful.* This is true. But so are most people with a lot on their minds.

Ms. Linda had hidden a key somewhere in her yard. But she couldn't remember where she'd hidden it. In fact, she had done this dozens of times. (She needed to remember to write it down—but of course, she'd forget this, too.)

Not wanting to be late for work, Ms. Linda hurried along the sidewalk. With no keys and no umbrella, she couldn't drive or protect herself from the rain, so she had to be fast. As she walked along quickly, she felt as though the scary storm cloud was following her. But that was unlikely...

...wasn't it?

The strange cloud crackled with purple electricity and then went *KRAK-KA-BOOM!* It shot a bolt of lightning right at Ms. Linda. It missed her by only a few inches.

"Yikes!" the teacher yelled, running as fast as she could.

As Ms. Linda ran into the school, she saw her boss. "I know, I know, I'm late!" she said.

The principal said, "No, you're not. You're actually early for once."

But Ms. Linda was still running. She ran down the hallway and into Classroom 13. She locked the door and closed the windows. The

thundercloud was still outside. She was sure it had followed her. So Ms. Linda did what any sensible person would do—she pulled down the blinds and pretended the cloud did not exist.

A few minutes later, there was a *knock knock knock* at the door.

"Ms. Linda, may I come inside the classroom?" Olivia asked from the hallway. "I would like to learn today."

"Oh! Yes, yes, of course, come in!" Ms. Linda said, unlocking the door.

"Why did you lock the door?" Olivia asked.

"A storm cloud followed me to school," Ms. Linda explained.

"That is highly unlikely," Olivia said.

"What's unlikely?" Mason asked, following Olivia into the classroom with his cow, Touchdown.

"Mason, what have I told you?" Ms. Linda said. "Touchdown has to stay outside. We already have a class pet. His name is Earl, and he is a gerbil."

"You mean *hamster*," Olivia corrected Ms. Linda.

"Is there a difference?" Ms. Linda asked.

"Gerbils have long furry tails. Hamsters do not," Olivia said. She was a bit of a know-it-all.

"Pleeeeease let me bring my cow inside," Mason begged the teacher. "There's a scary storm cloud outside, and Touchdown is scared."

"Fine," Ms. Linda said. "Touchdown may stay, as long as she does *not* disrupt class."

"How could a *cow* disrupt class?" Mason asked, rolling his eyes.

When the bell rang, the rest of the students rushed in to take their seats. Of Ms. Linda's twenty-seven students, all twenty-seven were present. Ms. Linda counted again to make sure that was correct. She asked, "Santiago, are you well enough to be in school?"

"Yes!" He sniffled, wiping his nose on his sleeve. "I refuse to miss another exciting day of school just because of a dumb little cold." Santiago was so pale, he was the same color as the chalk. When he sneezed, huge strands of neon-green snot came out of his nose.

"There's nothing exciting about school." Preeya yawned.

"There is in *this* classroom," Santiago said. "This class has won the lottery, made magic ~~genie~~ djinn wishes, and become famous!"

"And then we lost all of it," William reminded him. "I bet we're cursed."

"Being cursed would be exciting," Emma said.

"Well, it looks like we have a full day of class," Ms. Linda said. "We should probably get started. Today we'll be learning about—"

"Hold on. I'd like to return to our previous conversation," Olivia interrupted. She was smart, but she was also quite rude. "You said that the storm cloud outside the school *followed* you to

6

work. Could you please explain how and why a cloud would follow a person?"

"I have no idea. I'm a not a weather forecaster," Ms. Linda said. "But it did."

"Ms. Linda, really," Olivia said, shaking her head. "It's not like that thundercloud is hanging around outside the windows waiting for you—"

Triple J interrupted as he peeked outside. "Actually, it is."

The students rushed to the windows to see. "Students, no! Return to your seats at once!" Ms. Linda cried. But it was too late.

KRAK-KA-BOOOOOOOOM!

A huge bolt of purple lightning crashed through the window and struck everyone in Classroom 13.

It was lucky for Olivia that Ms. Linda was not the kind of person to say *I told you so*. Because if

she *was* that kind of person, she could have—and she would have been right in doing so. But Ms. Linda *wasn't* that kind of person, so she didn't say *I told you so*. (Though I, your honest author, Honest Lee, certainly would have.)

What's that? Oh, you want to know what happened to everyone? Don't worry. No one was hurt. Not yet, anyway...

CHAPTER 2
Super Ms. Linda

"**I**s everyone okay?" Ms. Linda asked, rubbing her head.

"Ms. Linda! You're flying!" Fatima said.

"And Santiago is on fire!" Ms. Linda screamed.

"*I'llputhimout!*" Teo said—but he said it so fast, no one understood. Teo grabbed the fire extinguisher and ran around Santiago sixteen times in one second, squirting him with the white powder.

Somehow, Santiago was still on fire—but he wasn't hurt. In fact, Santiago was laughing. Teo asked, "*WhyareyoulaughingandwhyamIsuperfast?*"

"I'm on fire, and it kind of tickles," Santiago said.

"*¿Qué pasó?*" Hugo asked.

"**EW! A GIANT SPIDER!**" Preeya said—except when she spoke, it was so loud, it shook the whole classroom like an earthquake.

"I'll kung-fu kick it!" Triple J said, rushing to the rescue. He was about to kick the eight-legged creature when it spoke.

"Don't kick me!" the boy-spider shrieked. "It's me, Dev!"

"What happened to everyone?!" Ms. Linda asked.

"Is it not evident? It certainly is to someone with my level of genius hyperintellect," Olivia said. Her brain was so huge it pushed out of her skull and glowed. "Caused by an alien solar flare from outer space, the electromagnetic storm cloud was filled with radioactive gamma rays that struck and transmuted our physical bodies into a higher form of energy-processing systems."

Everyone said, "Huh?" at the same time—that is, everyone except Fatima.

Fatima smiled bigger and harder than she'd ever smiled before. "Oh my gosh...can it be?...It's not possible...but it is!...It just happened....It's finally happened!"

"What happened?" Ms. Linda asked.

"It's just like Peter Powers's origin story in *Crazy Cool Comics* issue number eighty-nine," Fatima explained. "Some people get bitten by radioactive bugs, others are aliens who crash to Earth, and some—some are struck by weird lightning and get powers!"

"What on earth are you talking about?" Ms. Linda said.

Fatima took a deep breath and then shouted, "We all have *superpowers*!"

☆　　☆　　☆

"What a silly notion!" Ms. Linda said to herself as she walked home after work that day. "Sure, suddenly Ava can read minds and Benji can change size and Sophia can control the weather, but that's likely a coincidence. Being struck by lightning probably caused us to see things. Yes, that's it. It was all in our heads. Superpowers? Ridiculous! Fatima has been reading too many comic books."

(Dear reader, please note: There's *no* such thing as reading too many comic books. Comic books are fantastic fun.)

Suddenly, a mugger tried to snatch Ms. Linda's purse. Yet no matter how hard he yanked, he couldn't pull the purse from Ms. Linda's grip. "Stop that," she said. "This is my purse."

"Give it to me, old lady!" the thief growled. "Or else!"

"Old lady?!" Ms. Linda gasped. She only meant to slap the mugger for saying something so rude. Instead, she knocked him all the way across the street and into someone's car, smashing it.

The mugger fell to the ground and started crying. "That really hurt!"

"I didn't mean to slap you *that* hard," Ms. Linda said. She rushed over to help the mugger. She took his hand to help him up, but when she gripped it, she crushed every bone in his hand.

"OWWWWW!" the mugger screamed.

"Oh my!" Ms. Linda said. She tried to pick up the mugger and put him back on his feet. Instead, she tossed him into the air. "I didn't know I was so strong! I'm only trying to help."

"Stop helping!" the criminal cried. "What are you—some kind of superhero?!"

The teacher picked the mugger up with one hand and held him overhead. He was as light as a feather. "I guess I am," said Ms. Linda.

"Put me down!" the mugger screamed.

Ms. Linda didn't put him down until she was at the local police station. The cops clapped for Ms. Linda. "We've been trying to catch this guy for weeks. Thanks for the help!"

Classroom 13's resident teacher was not used to such praise—but she liked it. When Ms. Linda got home, she made herself a mask and a cape. That night, she went on patrol—which meant she went looking for trouble. When she found it, she fought it with her super-strength and stopped criminals from committing crimes.

That's when Ms. Linda began her double life. If she'd had her own comic book, it would have been titled: *Teacher by Day, Superhero by Night*.

Unfortunately, Ms. Linda had so much home-work to grade, she could only be a superhero on the weekends. And by the time Fridays rolled around, Ms. Linda was too tired to do superhero work. You see, teaching kids is a *lot* of work. After all, it is a huge responsibility and requires a lot of energy. So does being a superhero. In fact, they're pretty much the same thing. (Except instead of battling aliens and monsters, teachers battle bad grades and peanut allergies.)

So Ms. Linda had to make a choice—she could be a teacher *or* a superhero. She couldn't be both.

Ms. Linda thought long and hard. Finally, she decided to save her strength for her students. After only a few weeks as a superhero, Ms. Linda hung up her cape. Instead, she stayed home on the weekends to grade quizzes, watch Netflix, and eat cheese.

CHAPTER 3
Fatima

Fatima loved superhero comics.

So when everyone in Classroom 13 got super-powers, she thought her dreams had come true. Ximena could fly, Dev was a giant boy-spider, and Santiago was a human torch. Ava could read minds, Benji could shrink, and Teo was super-fast. But what was Fatima's power?

She tried to shoot laser blasts from her eyes. Nothing happened.

She tried to make objects move with her mind. Nothing happened.

She tried to transform into a monstrous hulk. Nothing happened.

She even tried to shoot a bow and arrow with perfect aim. (It wasn't exactly a superpower, but there was always an archer on every hero team in the comic books, so it was worth a shot.) But Fatima couldn't hit a target that was four feet away.

So what was her power?

It seemed she didn't have one.

Fatima's dream had become a nightmare.

CHAPTER 3 ½
Fatima & the Future

When Fatima got home from school, she was on the verge of tears. She ran upstairs and threw herself on her bed. As she screamed into her pillow, her superpower finally kicked in—she had a *vision of the future.*

It made sense. She always wanted to know what happened next in her favorite comics. Now she did. But this new power also showed her something terrible....

All of the superpowered students in Classroom 13 were fighting against one another with their superpowers. Some were heroes and some were villains, but all of them were angry. As they fought, their powers grew stronger and stronger until...

...they *broke the world in half!*

Fatima's vision ended. She couldn't see anything past that.

"They'll destroy the planet," she said. "I have to stop them! I have to save the world. But how?"

CHAPTER 4
Teo

Teo thought school was so slow. He was always in a hurry to get home and play video games. He stared at the clock and counted down the minutes.

That's when the purple lightning struck everyone in Classroom 13. Suddenly, Teo got superpowers that made him super-fast.

"*Holyguacamole,didyouseethat?IsavedSantiago's*

life,exceptIdidn'tbecausehe'sstillonfirebutIthinkhe's okay.Ithinkfireishissuperpower," Teo said.

"Teo, man, I have no idea what you're saying," Fatima said. "You're going to have to speak slower."

"Youcan'tunderstandme?" Teo asked. Fatima shook her head. Teo forced himself to speak as slowly as possible. But because he was speaking slowly very quickly, it came out normal. "How's this?"

"Much better!" Fatima answered. "Wow. You have super-speed. Why don't you run home and back and I'll time you?"

"Greatidea!Berightback!" Teo said. He ran home and then back to school again. Usually it took his mom fifteen minutes to drive him each way. Now, it took Teo only two seconds to run there and back.

"Holy guacamole, that was fast!" Fatima said. "You have to be the fastest person in the world."

"*That'sthecoolestthingever!*" Teo said. He'd never been a fan of actual exercise, but being the fastest boy alive? Pretty cool. He wanted to see just *how* fast he could go. "*I'mgoingtorun aroundtheworld!*" he told Fatima.

"Talk slower so I can understand you!" Fatima said.

"I'm going to run around the world," Teo said slowly. "See you later!" Teo vanished in a blur.

As he ran around the world, Teo visited the Great Wall of China, the Taj Mahal in India, the Kremlin in Russia, the Sydney Opera House in Australia, the Rio de Janeiro beaches in Brazil, the Leaning Tower of Pisa in Italy, Big Ben in England, Victoria Falls in Zimbabwe, and Mount Rushmore in South Dakota.

When he arrived back in Classroom 13, he asked Fatima, "How long have I been gone?"

She looked at her watch. "Seven minutes!"

Teo really was the fastest boy alive.

"Teo, please have a seat," Ms. Linda said. "You may have superpowers, but you are *not* excused from class."

Teo stared at the clock. It said 2:37. After what felt like hours and hours and hours, it still said 2:37.

"Why is time moving so slowly?" he asked Fatima.

"Well, now that you're super-fast, every second will seem like days," Fatima explained. "Time moves slower when you're super-fast."

Dramatically, Teo shouted, "*Noooooooooooooo!*"

CHAPTER 5
Ava

Have you ever wanted to know what other people are thinking? I promise—you really don't.

Ava, Preeya, and Zoey used to be best friends. But lately, Preeya and Zoey had been ignoring Ava. Preeya and Zoey even made weird faces at Ava. The worst part for Ava was that she didn't know why. When Ava was struck by lightning, all she wanted was to know what they were whispering about.

And now she had the power to read people's minds.

The first thing Ava did with her new power was peek inside her friends' heads. They were furious with Ava for not inviting them to her birthday party.

"I didn't have a birthday party!" Ava explained. "I was sick."

"Really?" Zoey said. She and Preeya weren't mad at Ava anymore. They were all friends again. Yay!

(Yes, I know. Their situation seems silly, but hurt feelings can make people act irrational.)

Only now Ava knew exactly what *everyone* was thinking.

At first, Ava used her gift to help her fellow classmates. She helped Chloe remember where she'd left her favorite coat. She helped William remember his grandparents' birthdays. She even helped Ms. Linda remember where she'd put her keys—under the potted plant on her porch.

But as time went on, Ava couldn't help but hear everything that the boys in class were thinking. All Mark thought about was corn chips. (Odd.) All Liam thought about was farts. (Yuck.) And all Dev and Teo and Triple J thought about were the horrible and violent video games they loved to play. (So gross.)

Boys are weird, Ava thought. She did not like hearing their thoughts. So she tried to pay attention to only the girls in class.

But theirs weren't much better. All Olivia thought about was good grades. (Strange.) All Isabella thought about was horse poop. (Nasty.) And all Preeya and Zoey thought about was how dumb Ava's new haircut was. (So mean!)

Girls are just as bad as boys, Ava thought. She stormed over to Preeya and Zoey and yelled, "I love my haircut! I don't care what you think!"

"Ms. Linda!" Zoey called, raising her hand. "Ava is reading our minds without our permission!"

"Ava, please stop, or I'll have to give you detention," Ms. Linda said.

Ava no longer liked her power. In fact, she hated it. You might think hearing other people's thoughts is a super superpower, but it is not. It's awful. Can you imagine having other people's thoughts in your own head? After a while, you may not know whose thoughts are whose—including yours.

CHAPTER 6
Mason

Every day, Mason walked home after school. Today, he wondered what his superpower was. He thought it would be cool to make milk. Then he remembered that's why he had a pet cow.

Mason tried to remember what he had been thinking about when the lightning struck. He couldn't remember. He wondered if he would grow tiger fur, or shoot fireworks out of his fingers, or turn into a fly and fly away. None of that happened. Instead, he vanished!

One second he was in front of the school—the next second, he was in front of his house. Naked!

"Yikes!" he screamed. He ran inside and locked the door. He looked out the window to see if anyone had seen him. "How did I get home?" he wondered out loud. He didn't remember walking home. He also didn't remember taking off his clothes.

Mason knew he wasn't the smartest kid around, so he guessed that he'd just forgotten walking home and getting naked. "Oh well," he said. He got dressed and went to bed. (Yes, it was still afternoon, but like I said, Mason wasn't the smartest kid around.)

In the middle of the night, Mason had a dream that he visited the pyramids of Egypt. Several tourists looked at him and said, "That little boy is naked!"

Mason woke up and said, "What a horrible dream!" But the odd part? There was *sand* in his bed.

The next morning, Mason got dressed for school. He had some toast and was thinking about what he would (or wouldn't) learn in school that day. And suddenly he was there—in Classroom 13. Once again, he was naked.

"Why does this keep happening to me?" he screamed. Luckily, it was early, so no one was at school yet. He grabbed a coat from the lost and found, put it on, then ran home.

"Mom, I keep disappearing and reappearing somewhere else," Mason said.

"Of course you do, dear," she said, sipping her coffee slowly. She was not a morning person.

Mason walked very slowly to school. He watched each footstep, making sure not to think about other places. When he got to school, he grabbed Fatima and yelled, "I don't like my superpower! It makes me naked!"

"Hold on," Fatima said. "Start at the beginning and tell me everything." So Mason did. Fatima knew what his power was. "So cool! You're a teleporter!"

"Is that like a telephone?" Mason asked. "Or a telescope?"

"No, a teleporter means you travel from one place to another *instantly*. You don't need a car or a plane or a boat. You just think about somewhere and you're there!"

Mason thought about Hawaii. Instantly, he was there on a Hawaiian beach. He was also naked. "Ack!" he screamed. Then he teleported back to Classroom 13. He was still naked.

Fatima picked up his clothes and handed them to him. "It seems that when you teleport, you can only teleport yourself. That means you can't teleport with a friend, or with your cow, or even with clothes. You can travel anywhere—just naked."

"That's a crummy superpower," Mason said.

"No, the power is super cool," Fatima noted. "It's the naked thing that's super crummy."

"How do I turn it off?" Mason asked.

"I don't think you can," Fatima said. "You just have to learn how to control it."

For the next few hours, Mason tried to control his thoughts: He tried *not* to think about other places.

(I don't know about you, dear reader, but the more I try *not* to think about something, the more I think about it. For instance, if I told you, *"Don't think about strawberries,"* what would you think about?

Exactly! You think about *strawberries*. Now stop thinking about strawberries and get back to Mason's story.)

By lunchtime, Mason was so stressed out about not teleporting, he lost his appetite. Instead of eating, all he could think about was teleporting somewhere, naked, and getting in trouble. "You have to stop thinking about it," Triple J said. "Otherwise you'll end up somewhere bad. Like the principal's office."

As soon as Triple J said it, Mason thought of Principal Pumpernickel's office. Instantly, there he was, sitting on the principal's desk. Naked.

"Mason Mathers Marshall! What do you think you're doing?!" Principal Pumpernickel shouted.

"It wasn't me!" Mason protested. "It's my superpower! I can't help it!"

"Your superpower is being naked and putting your butt on my desk? That doesn't make any sense!" the principal barked. Mr. Pumpernickel gave Mason his jacket to cover up. "Consider yourself in deep, deep, *deep* trouble, Mr. Marshall. I am calling your mother. You'll be in detention for the rest of your days!"

"Crummiest superpower ever," Mason muttered to himself.

Mason thought his trouble was over. When he went home, he was so upset, he'd lost his appetite. Mason never skipped dessert, but tonight he did. Instead, he kept drinking water. Eventually, all he could think about was peeing, and he really had to go. He excused himself and ran to the bathroom.

As he started to go, he immediately felt relaxed—so relaxed that he closed his eyes and let his mind drift. A random thought popped into his head—what if he got into trouble with the police?

The sound of pee splashing in the toilet changed to the sound of pee splashing on a policeman's boot. When Mason opened his eyes, he was no longer at home. He was in a police station, peeing on the police chief's boot. Once again, Mason was naked.

The police threw him in jail.

"You're in big trouble!" they shouted. But

without an ID, they had no way to identify Mason. (Though he wasn't very smart, Mason *was* smart enough *not* to tell them his name.)

Don't worry. Mason wasn't in jail for very long. Unfortunately for the cops, no jail cell could hold Mason. Of course, neither could clothes.

CHAPTER 7
Chloe

*You might think I forgot to write Chloe's chapter—but I didn't. You see, Chloe got the power of invisibility. So that's how I wrote the chapter— invisibly. You're welcome.

CHAPTER 8
Santiago

What happens to a superhero when they're *super* sick? Ask Santiago.

Santiago had the worst cold. All he wanted was to warm up. And now...well, he's actually burning up. Like, for real. As in, he burned a hole in the desk just sitting there. (I don't own a thermometer, but he's got to be running three thousand degrees hotter than most kids.)

You see, the super cloud that gave everyone in Classroom 13 superpowers had given Santiago *pyro*-powers—which meant he could make and control *fire*.

As ~~cool~~ *hot* as that sounds, it didn't do much for Santiago's horrible cold. Instead of sneezing snot out of his nose, he sneeze-blasted fireballs straight through his box of tissues.

"Extra-strength tissue?!" Santiago said, reading the Kleenex box label. "S'NOT!"

Every time Santiago sneezed, something in the 13th Classroom caught on fire. Ms. Linda (and the local fire department) was getting tired of putting out the little fires. "Young man, I am happy you felt well enough to come to school today, but I am calling your mother. I must insist she take you home," Ms. Linda said.

But Santiago didn't want to miss school. Every time Santiago missed a day of class in Classroom 13, something *unlucky* or *disastrous* or *terrible* happened. And he didn't want to miss anything—be it super or awful! Especially not when everyone had superpowers.

"Hold on, Ms. Linda," Santiago said. "There must be some way for me to control my powers. Let me try something...." He held his breath and sat perfectly still. Slowly, his flames died down.

"There," he said breathlessly. "I just won't breathe. No more fire. You won't even know I'm...I'm..."

But as we all know, you can't hold in a sneeze.

"Aa-aa-AA-CHOOOOO!!!" Santiago sneezed such a huge fireball, it punched a hole right through the 13th Classroom's wall.

"I'm sorry, Santiago. You are sick," Ms. Linda said. "You must go home."

Santiago's mom drove to school and picked him up—then took him to the fire department. They put him in a fireproof suit. While all his classmates and friends were out and about using their superpowers in the real world, Santiago was forced to return home and miss out on all the fun. Again.

His mom brought him a bowl of chicken soup. He tasted it. "It's cold!"

"So heat it up," his mom said.

Santiago took off his fireproof gloves and boiled the soup in his blazing hands. He hated being sick. It made him *steaming* angry.

CHAPTER 9
Yuna

You might be wondering: "Where's Yuna?"

Or: "What's her superpower?"

Or: "What's her story?"

~~Or (most likely): "Wah! I need a nap!"~~ Ignore that. That was *me* wondering that. What were we talking about? Oh, yes: Yuna!

I know all about Yuna, but she said I could only tell you in Morse code:

-•-- ••- -• •- / •••• •- -•• / •- •-••

•-- •- -•-- ••• / •-- •- -•-• - • -•• /

- --- / -••• • / •- / ••• •--• -•--

•-•-• / ••• --- / •-- •••• • -• / •••

•••• • / --• --- - / •••• • •-• / •---

--- •-- • •-• ••• --••-- / ••• •••• •

/ -•-• --- •-- •-•• -•• / •-- •- •-••

-•- / - •••• •-• --- ••- --• •••• /

•-- •- •-•• •- •-• ••• / •-•• •• -•- • /

•- / --• •••• --- ••• - •-•-• / •-- ••

- •••• / - •••• •• ••• / •- -••• •• •-••

•• - -•-- --••-- / ••• •••• • / -•-•

--- ••- •-•• -•• / -••• • -•-• --- -- •

/ •- / ••• ••- •--• • •-• ••• •--• -•--

•-•-• / -• --- / •-•• --- -•-• •- - •

-•• / -•• --- --- •-• / -•-• --- ••-

•-•• -•• / ••• - --- •--• / •••• • •-• /

-• --- •-- •-•-• / - --- --- / -••• •

-•• / •••• • •-• / •--• --- •-- • •-•

••• / •-- --- ••- •-•• -•• -• -• •----• - /

•-•• •- ••• - •-•-•-

CHAPTER 10
Jayden Jason

Fatima had been jotting down notes about all of her classmates. She approached Jayden Jason James—aka Triple J, aka the Most Popular Kid in Class—and asked, "So what's your power?"

"I'm not sure," he said.

"Try to do something," Fatima suggested.

Triple J felt sudden strength in his muscles. With one swift chop, he broke his desk in half.

When he jump-kicked, he flew into the air. When he punched, he hit with the force of a thousand ninja warriors inside his fist.

"I've got super *kung fu*!" Triple J said.

"Actually, that's karate," Fatima said.

Triple J shrugged. "Whatever."

That night, Triple J put his superhero costume together. He went to the local mall and bought a karate *gi* (that's the name for the uniform in Japanese). Then he tied a headband around his forehead. He also renamed himself Jay-Fu. Jay-Fu planned to fight crime and protect the people in his neighborhood.

The only problem? Jay-Fu lived in a really nice, safe community.

Instead of chasing down villains on rooftops, Jay-Fu chased cats out of trees. Instead of stopping armored car heists, Jay-Fu fixed flat tires. Instead of battling bat monsters and boogeymen, Jay-Fu battled being bored.

The fact was, his neighborhood didn't need a superpowered hero.

Jay-Fu skulked back to his house feeling useless. His mom was making dinner—spaghetti and meatballs. Jay-Fu was about to toss his *gi* in the trash when he saw she needed help.

"I can't get this jar of sauce open!" his mom said. "Pasta night will be ruined!"

With the mysterious Ancient Spinning Palm technique, Jay-Fu opened the pasta sauce jar with ease.

A smile blossomed on his mom's face. She cried, "Jayden, you're my hero!"

Jay-Fu took an honorable bow. "You may thank my powerful kung fu."

"Actually, that was karate," she said. Then his mom sat him down and gave him a long talk about the differences between martial arts. Not even a superpowered ~~kung fu~~ karate hero can stand against a mother's lecture.

CHAPTER 11
Preeya

Preeya felt like no one ever listened to her. In class, she talked and talked and talked, and Ms. Linda was always saying things like, "Preeya, please be quiet during my lesson," or, "Preeya, no talking during tests."

It was the same at home. Her brother always said, "Preeya, quit talking during my TV shows." Her dad always said, "Preeya, hush. I'm on a work call." Her older sister—who she shared a room with—always said, "Preeya, I'm doing my homework. *Shhhh.*" Why didn't anyone ever listen to Preeya?!

Of course, once she got her powers, they didn't have a choice. If people thought she was loud before (which they did), nothing could prepare them for her new *superpowerful* voice.

"What's wrong with my voice?" she asked. But it was so LOUD, it blew out the classroom windows. Every eye in Classroom 13 was on Preeya—including all eight of Dev's spider eyes.

"No more talking, Preeya!" Ms. Linda said. "You'll wreck the school!"

Preeya clapped her hands over her mouth. When she got home, she didn't say anything. She watched TV with her family, but she was too scared to speak. But at dinner, her mom asked, "How was school today, dear?"

Preeya shook her head.

"Don't be rude, Preeya. Answer your mother," her dad said.

"It was weird," she said. Her voice was so powerful, it knocked over the kitchen table and blasted her family out of their chairs.

"What is going on?!" her father shouted. "Preeya, explain this instant!"

Preeya shook her head.

"If you don't tell us, you're grounded!" her mother insisted.

Not wanting trouble, she answered, **"I got superpowers**." Her voice exploded the fridge and the dishwasher.

"You are grounded, young lady!" her mother shouted.

"But you *made* me speak!" Preeya yelled. Her yell was even more powerful—it blasted a hole in their kitchen wall.

"Not another word!" her father growled.

Preeya was furious. Even with superpowers, no one wanted to listen to her.

Of course, if she were a super-*villain*, they would *have* to listen. Preeya smiled mischievously....

CHAPTER 12
Mark

Mark was unbearably handsome. Everyone in Classroom 13 thought so (even the 13th Classroom agreed). So when everyone got superpowers, everyone was curious what superpowers Mark would get.

At the time of the lightning strike, Mark was thinking of one thing: salty corn chips. He loved salt and he loved corn chips. He could eat them day and night. He could eat them for breakfast, lunch, and dinner. He liked them plain, or with yogurt, or with cheese—as long as they were salty.

So what powers did he get? Well, he got the power to *control* corn chips.

What does that mean? Well, if you control metal, it's like you have magnet powers: You can move metal in the air, and bend metal, and make metal do whatever you want. Mark's powers worked the same way: He could move corn chips in the air, and bend corn chips (which would break), and make corn chips do whatever he wanted.

Mostly, he made corn chips fly into his mouth.

Every once in a while, he helped his friends fight crime. You might be wondering how?

Well, when Mark saw a robber robbing a bank, or a bully bullying someone smaller, he used his control over chips to make them fling salt into the villain's eyes.

Have you ever gotten salt in your eye?

It really hurts.

If you *haven't* gotten salt in your eyes—good for you.

If you *have*—then you know what I'm talking about.

What's that? Why would I put salt in my eyes? I didn't do it on purpose! I was eating chips. Salty, delicious corn chips.

Mmmm. Why do they have to be so darn delicious?

CHAPTER 13
The 13th Classroom

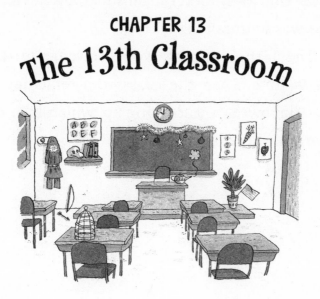

When the students of Classroom 13 were struck by lightning, the Classroom laughed out loud. (Of course, no one heard the Classroom over the thunder outside.)

But when the students turned out to be okay and not hurt at all—and, in fact, had been given *superpowers*—the 13th Classroom was more furious than ever. It had always wanted to be a

superhero. Why didn't it get superpowers, too?! This was so unfair!

The 13th Classroom vowed revenge for the *fourth* time. Then the Classroom remembered that Halloween was coming up, which inspired a terrible, horrible, nasty idea....

CHAPTER 14
Lily

Lily had always wanted to travel into outer space so that she could explore new worlds. But when she got her superpowers, she discovered another way to see new worlds—all she had to do was step sideways and walk into other dimensions.

You see, there is *not* just one dimension—there are lots of them. One dimension is a world where dinosaurs still live and have to go to school

just like you. Another is a place where everyone can do magic, so everyone thinks magic is dumb and boring. One dimension has robots that have taken over and enslaved the human race. There's even a world where potatoes are the most intelligent life-form on the planet.

One dimension is the one where Classroom 13 exists. And then there is *your* dimension, where you are reading about Classroom 13 right now.

Anyway. Using her new powers, Lily stepped sideways and walked into the next dimension. (Instead of forward or backward, she walked to the left). The school looked like hers, except there was no Classroom 13. There was a Classroom 12 and a Classroom 14, but no 13.

She was about to leave when a young boy said, "Where did you come from?"

"Another dimension," Lily explained. "I just got superpowers that allow me to walk through different dimensions."

"Cool! I have superpowers, too, but they're kinda lame," he said. "My name is Peter Powers, and I can...*ugh*, this is really embarrassing....I can make ice cubes with my fingertips."

"You're right," Lily said. "That power *is* pretty lame."

"Hey, I can make drinks cold!" Peter said.

"Good for you," Lily said.

Peter Powers is a real kid in a real book series that you can read...for real. It's written by some silly guy named Kent Clark. He and Honest Lee once had a super-battle. Kent Clark lost.

CHAPTER 15
Ethan

If you had superpowers, what would you choose: superhero or super-villain? Good or evil? Underwear on the inside or the *outside* of your super-suit?

For most people, the choice would be simple. But not for Ethan.

He could never make up his mind. Even the tiniest decision could take him weeks to decide. Like the time he stopped eating because he couldn't choose between a hamburger or a cheeseburger. Well, now that he had super-powers, he faced the biggest decision of his life: hero or villain.

"What's your power, anyway?" Fatima asked.

"I'm a super-smart robot inventor," Ethan answered.

"That sounds so lame!" said Liam.

"I think it's cool. While you've been inside farting, I've been outside building *THAT*." Ethan pointed to a giant robot on the playground. It was taller than the school. "It has lasers, shields, and rocket launchers, and can transform into a spaceship. It also has a soft-serve ice-cream machine in the cockpit."

"RAD!" Liam freaked. "What flavor?!"

"I can never decide." Ethan frowned. "So I put in chocolate *and* vanilla."

"Dude, that is awesome," Dev whispered.

"Look, don't tell anyone, but I'm putting together a super-villain team. You should totally join."

"Can I think about it?" Ethan asked. But after hours and hours, he still couldn't decide. His mom suggested he put together a pros and cons list. So he did:

SHOULD I BE A SUPER-VILLAIN?

PROS	CONS
Villains have more fun...	...except when they're in jail.
Villains don't follow rules...	...probably have mean parents.
Villains have cooler weapons...	...heroes have better friends.
When villains die, they come back...	...but heroes just beat them up again.

Days went by. Ethan still couldn't decide. So instead of making a decision, he decided *not* to make a decision.

Instead, Ethan and his forty-foot robot went to the beach with his family. They had a very fun time in the sun.

CHAPTER 16
Isabella

When Isabella found out she might have a superpower, she was excited to beat up bad guys. But even more than that, she hoped she'd become a horse. Or maybe a centaur, which is a half-person, half-horse. I mean, she really *loved* horses—so much that she was sure she would have some kind of *horse-power*.

As she raced to the girls' bathroom to look for a mirror, she couldn't stop thinking about how awesome she would be as a horse: Her mane would be flowing and pretty. Her horseshoes would be shiny and new. And she would be the most feared crime-fighting horse out there. She'd kick crime in the butt—with her hooves!

Of course, when she saw herself in a mirror, she *flippered* out.

"A dolphin?!" she screamed. Isabella had no horse-power of any kind. Instead, she'd changed into an aquatic mammal. She was *not* happy. But she only had herself to blame. When the lightning struck, she obviously hadn't been thinking about horses.

She would've been happier as a sea horse. But a dolphin? It was just a big ~~dumb~~ smart ~~fish~~ dolphin.

At least she could stand up straight, breathe normal air, and talk. That meant she could still go to class, birthday parties, and...well, maybe not aquatic shows.

As for superhero battles and crime-fighting? *Dolphin*-ately not.

CHAPTER 17
Hugo

*H*ugo sólo hablaba francés, es decir, hasta que todos en el Aula 13 tuvieran superpoderes.

¿Cuál era su? ¡Ahora sólo podía hablar español! Que embarazoso. Lo sé. Es un superpotencia terrible. Mientras sus amigos estaban volando o luchando contra villanos o salvando al mundo, todo lo que Hugo podía hacer era hablar un idioma diferente.

¿La peor parte? Sus padres no podían entender nada de lo que decía. Hugo quería pizza para la cena. En cambio, tenían tacos.

Hugo odiaba los tacos.

CHAPTER 18
Mya & Madison

Mya & Madison were identical twins. They thought alike, talked alike, and looked alike. Though they didn't have to, they also dressed alike. If Mya wore a blue dress, Madison did, too. If Madison wore green shoes, so did Mya. If Mya put her hair in a ponytail, Madison did the same. And if Madison...You get the picture.

But that morning, something terrible

happened—Mya & Madison wore (are you ready for this?) *different outfits*!!

Madison wore blue jeans and a yellow shirt, and Mya wore a red dress with flowers on it.

You see, they woke up late, got dressed in a hurry, and didn't realize their clothes weren't matching until they were on the way to school.

"Dad, stop the car!" Mya yelled.

"We need to go home and change our clothes to match!" Madison added.

"Absolutely not," their father said. "I'm late for work. You can dress *not* alike for one day."

"No, we can't!" they screamed. Their father ignored them.

The girls were feeling sorry for themselves when the purple lightning struck. Well, thanks to their new powers, they could look *however* they wanted. They were shapeshifters.

What's a shapeshifter? It's someone who can change their appearance just by thinking about it.

I'm not talking about disguises; I'm talking about someone who can instantly change their face and body to *become* a totally different person whenever they want. Imagine: You could change your hair color to neon orange. You could change your eye color to bloodred. You could change your skin color to glitter green.

You could turn into the queen of England, or a giant lion, or an alien space robot. You could become a giant dinosaur, or a bald eagle, or you could look like your favorite TV star. You could change into a banana, or a book, or a boat. That's what a shapeshifter can do. They can change into *anything*!

And what, or *who*, do you think Mya & Madison morphed into? Hmmm? Two Ms. Lindas? Two Abe Lincolns? Two world-famous *super*models?

Nope.

All the twins did was shapeshift their outfits to match. And they were happy with that.

CHAPTER 19
Jacob

Jacob didn't get a superpower. When the purple lightning struck his classmates and teacher, he was in the bathroom.

☹

CHAPTER 20
Emma

You know how Isabella feels about horses? Well, Emma feels the same way about cats. She loves loves LOVES cats. Her whole life, all Emma had wanted was a pet cat. There were just two things in the way:

1. She was *super*-allergic to them, and
2. Her mom and dad. Though they were divorced, both agreed on one thing: "I'll

never have a filthy, flea-ridden feline in my home!" (Their words, not mine.)

Emma used to be annoyed with her parents' anti-cat ways—but now she was terrified she'd be homeless. With her soft coat, her whiskers, and her tail, there was no way her parents would let her in either of their houses....

Oh, did I forget to explain? The strange thundercloud with the purple lightning changed Emma into a GIRL-CAT.

"Oh no. Does this mean I'm allergic *to myself*?!" Emma said in a panic. She licked her paw to be sure. No hives. No rash. Well, that was good.

Being a cat may not sound so superpowerish, but I assure you it is. Thanks to her new cat features, Emma could smell danger (and tuna fish) from blocks away. She had razor-sharp fangs (and bad kitten breath). Thanks to her claws, she could climb walls and trees. She had fast reflexes and always landed on her feet (though she *was* easily distracted by feathers on strings).

"Hey, Girl-Cat, me and some of the other heroes are going to hit the streets for a patrol. Want to join?" ~~Jay-Fu~~ Triple J asked.

Emma yawned. "Thanks, but no thanks, Jay-Fu. I need a catnap. Licking oneself all day is exhausting."

Emma was worried about how her parents would react when they saw her. She decided her dad was a little nicer, so she went to his place first. "Are you house-trained?" he asked.

"Of course!" she said.

He let her stay—until she knocked books off bookshelves, scratched up his sofa, and shed all over the rug. "Bad kitty, *er*, I mean...bad *daughter!*" her dad said. "Out you go! Shoo!"

So Emma went to her mom's house. Her mom let her in, gave her a hug, and put down a saucer of milk. But just like a real cat, Emma soon hid somewhere in the house. No matter how many times her mom shook the bag of treats, Emma wouldn't come out until she was ready.

CHAPTER 21
Benji

No one had seen or heard from Benji Bearenstein for days. Ms. Linda and her students were worried. So were Benji's parents. The police put together a search party, and the superheroes of Classroom 13 were looking everywhere (when they weren't doing their homework).

At the end of the week, Ms. Linda was beside herself. She had been the last person to see Benji, right before the lightning struck. Where could he be?

Ms. Linda felt something on the back of her hand. She thought it was an ant until she realized it was tap-dancing. Then it jumped up and down and waved at her. It looked like...but it couldn't be...

Ms. Linda grabbed a magnifying glass from her desk drawer and looked through it. She gasped. "BENJI!?!"

"Hey, Ms. Linda!" his voice squeaked. Benji was tiny. His superpower shrank him down to itty-bitty-teensy-weensy.

Ms. Linda was both shocked and horrified, but Benji didn't mind it so much. He'd always loved miniature things. When he was normal size, he drank juice from doll-sized teacups. He sharpened his pencils down to tiny nubs so he could have the *littlest* writing utensils. He even started a miniature animal business once (but that's a whole other story you probably already know if you knew Benji when he won the lottery).

For Benji, being *tiny* was the **biggest** thing that had ever happened—so he'd been having fun.

It turns out when you're super small, everything else is super big. That meant traveling across Classroom 13 didn't take seconds, it took *days*. Desks were as high as mountains, books were as big as buildings, and specks of dust rolled around like giant tumbleweeds.

Cockroaches were the size of trucks and they were *not* nice when they thought you were dinner. Mini-Benji had barely survived by learning to use a broken staple as a sword. He'd also befriended a group of ants (each the size of a horse) who led him to a pile of corn chip crumbs underneath Mark's desk. He'd never been so grateful for someone's leftovers.

Mini-Benji told Ms. Linda all of this while

she fed him water through an eyedropper. (One drop was like a giant waterfall for Benji.) As he drank, he began to grow—though not much. As soon as he reached six inches tall, he stopped growing. His parents came to pick him up and his mom cried all the way home. But his little sister couldn't have been happier. She let him live inside her dollhouse as long as he agreed to be nice to Barbie.

CHAPTER 22
Sophia

Sophia wanted to save the planet. That's why she'd started the school's recycling program, spent her weekends planting trees, and picked up litter for fun. She didn't need a cape to be a hero—just the desire to keep planet Earth as green as possible.

Before the purple lightning struck, Sophia was gazing outside. It hadn't rained in weeks and the grass outside was turning brown. So when Sophia got powers, it just so happened that she could control the weather.

The first thing she did? Made it rain. When the plants were all watered, Sophia said, "That's enough!" Then a huge wind came and pushed the clouds over to the next town.

"Amazing!" Ava said.

"That's the coolest power ever!" ~~Jay-Fu~~ Triple J said.

But Fatima warned, "That's a really big ability—be careful how you use it. Or else..."

Sophia shrugged, ignoring Fatima's advice.

That week was the best of Sophia's life. She could create miniature rain clouds to shower her garden. She could make a gentle breeze to blow dust off her indoor plants. And she could make little lightning bolts to zap her annoying brother in the butt.

When Sophia was happy, the sun shined

bright outside. When she read a sad story, it would get cold and gray. If she got angry (usually because of her brother), the wind would get so wild, it'd knock down all the trash cans in her neighborhood. It even knocked down a few streetlights.

Sophia's weather powers got so strong that when she watched a sad movie and started crying, it began to storm outside. The problem was, Sophia *loved* sad movies. If it was a tearjerker, she'd watch it. She loved to cry.

But it all turned bad on Saturday when she decided to have a sad movie marathon. At first, the weather was just foggy and drizzling. Then it began to rain. Soon, it began to hail. Then the storm turned into a full-fledged flash flood. At this rate, the town would be completely underwater by the end of the night.

Fatima rowed a boat over to Sophia's house. She climbed through Sophia's window and unplugged her TV.

"Hey, I was watching that!" Sophia moaned.

"Have you looked outside?" Fatima asked. "Your weather powers are connected to your feelings. And your sad movie marathon is destroying the town!"

"Oh no, the plants!" Sophia said. Outside the window, entire trees were floating down the river that had been her driveway. She started to cry.

"Stop!" Fatima shouted. "You need to control your emotions."

"Okay," Sophia said. "But how?"

Fatima thought for a moment. "Do your homework?"

"Perfect!" Sophia said. "Homework doesn't make me happy or sad. It just makes me bored."

CHAPTER 23
Dev

Every day after school, Dev walked into his house and said, "Mom, I'm home!" This was usually her cue to give him a kiss on the forehead and make him a snack.

Today, his mom did *not* kiss him on the forehead. Instead, she screamed in terror. Then she chased him around the living room with a rolled-up newspaper, trying to smash him. After

Dev explained everything, she calmed down. Mostly.

Dev had become a spider-boy. He had eight limbs, eight eyes, and the ability to make webs. Strangely (or perhaps not so strangely), his mother, Mrs. Darsha, had a hard time dealing with this.

Every time she saw Dev come around the corner, she nearly had a heart attack. There was a child-sized arachnid in her house, and her bug-killing instincts kept kicking in. You see, Mrs. Darsha prided herself on keeping a very clean home. When she saw something with more than four legs, she wanted to kill it.

When Spider-Dev bumped into her in the hallway, she took off her shoe and tried to smash him.

When Spider-Dev joined the family for dinner, she tried to smash him with a frying pan.

When Spider-Dev joined her on the couch for movie night, she sprayed him with bug spray.

"Mom, that burns!" he screamed.

"Well," she said, "it serves you right, you hideous monster—uh, I mean, my beautiful son."

Finally, Dev figured out a way to avoid his mom. He crawled around on the ceiling just out of Mrs. Darsha's reach.

The worst part of the whole thing? Dev had *wanted* to become a spider-boy. He thought having eight limbs would mean he could play four video games at the same time. Unfortunately, it turns out spiders don't have thumbs.

VACUUM MAN! WE SHOULD HAVE KNOWN!
HAHA! LOOKY HERE. IT'S FART FORCE!
THAT'S FUR FORCE, PAL.
UUM MAN
YOU'RE TOO LATE, BLUNDERPETS. I'VE ALREADY VACUUMED UP THE JEWELS!
AND HOW ARE YOU GONNA STOP ME? YOU GONNA WHISKER ME TO DEATH?
AND YOU ... WHAT ARE YOU GONNA DO? HIT ME WITH EXPIRED MILK?! HAHAHA!
GRRRR!!!
ANGRY!
WE DON'T NEED FISTS.
WE'RE GONNA USE OUR WORDS!
THE SUPERPOWER OF SPEECH BUBBLES!
TD

THEY HAD USED UP ALL THEIR WORDS!

CLASS PET

DO NOT FEED PIZZA!

LIAM WAS HERE X

MOO!

AND WENT BACK TO NORMAL

EARL COULD ONLY SQUEAK, TOUCHDOWN COULD ONLY MOO. BUT THE CITY WOULD BE TALKING ABOUT THEIR HEROIC DEEDS FOREVER.

JAIL

N13

VACUUM MAN IS IN JAIL THANKS TO TWO MYSTERY HEROES. NEWS 13 AND THIS CITY, THANK THEM.

PIZZA

HEROES

WHAAAA? I KNOW THOSE DUDES!

CHAPTER 25
Ximena

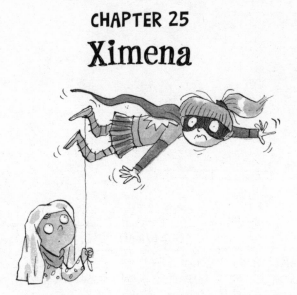

When you ask someone, "If you could have any superpower, what would it be?" nine out of ten people will answer, "I wish I could fly."

Ximena was one of those people. When she got her power, she became lighter than air. She floated up from her desk and touched the ceiling. She kicked off the walls and made a loop around the room, never touching the ground. She could *fly!*

She said to herself, "Best power ever!"

"Cool!" Ava said.

"I wish I could fly," Mark moaned.

"*Thatpowerisawesome*," Teo said really fast.

"Neat-o!" Mason said. "Hey! Can you get my paper airplane? It's stuck in the air vent."

"Can't you just teleport up there?" she asked.

"I could, but then I'd be naked," he said.

"No worries, I'll get it," Ximena said. But when she tried to fly forward, she jump-flipped backward and bumped her head. "That's odd. I can't seem to control where I'm going."

"You're like a bird. You just need more room," Chloe said. She opened the window. Ximena kicked off the ceiling and flew outside.

But as soon as she went through the window, she started floating up, up, and away. Ximena couldn't control herself. She was like a balloon, flying higher and higher into the sky. "Help!" she shouted.

The students from Classroom 13 ran after her. Luckily, a big gust of wind blew her down from the sky and closer to the ground. Ximena spun through the air. The wind sent her in loop-de-loops, causing her to bump her head on traffic lights and scuff her knees on lampposts. Eventually, the wind blew her into a tree where she got stuck in the branches long enough for her classmates to come rescue her.

It was Fatima's idea to tie some rope around Ximena's ankle and hold on to her like a balloon. It turned out she couldn't exactly fly so much as float. Fatima pulled Ximena back to Classroom 13. When they were safely inside, she let her go. Ximena fluttered up and bounced on the ceiling.

"I stand corrected," Ximena said to herself. "Worst power ever."

CHAPTER 26
~~William~~
The Incredible Bulk

William was paranoid. He didn't trust anybody. He thought that "homework" was an elaborate prank Ms. Linda played on him each day. While he was home doing math and spelling, he believed everyone else was having a pizza party.

So when the purple lightning hit the classroom, William thought it was another fake-out.

William certainly couldn't remember having any amazing abilities...

...though there was something strange going on.

Every day—just before lunchtime—William would start to get a headache. Then he'd black out. When he'd wake up, he'd be in some strange new place surrounded by fish and destruction. His clothes would be torn, and he'd have no memory of what had happened. He was certain his class was playing a cruel joke on him.

"Not cool, you guys!" he said to them.

"William, it's not a joke," ~~Jay-Fu~~ Triple J said. William didn't believe him.

"You really do have superpowers," Ms. Linda insisted. William didn't believe her.

"It's true," his grandparents explained. "We made a video of it." William refused to watch the video. He didn't even believe his grandparents.

But it was completely true.

As you know, every day—just before lunchtime—William would start to get a headache. But what really happened when he blacked out was this: His body grew huge and turned bright green. He'd beat his chest in a rage and shout, "I am Bulk! Bulk is hungry! Bulk want fish sticks!"

Then he would blaze a path of destruction in his search for fish sticks. The first time it happened, he destroyed the school's cafeteria. The second time, he used a school bus as a baseball bat and attacked the local pier. And the third time, he wrecked the downtown district of the nearest city.

But when he finally ate fish sticks, he'd fall asleep, shrink, and turn back to normal. When William would wake, he'd have no memory of being the Incredible Bulk (which is what the news called the hungry monster).

William didn't believe it, but it was true. It was all true.

"Yeah, right," William said. "Honestly, Honest Lee, I thought you'd be honest with me."

"What? You can hear me?" I (your author) said to William.

"Of course I can hear you," William said, "and I know you're talking behind my back."

"I wouldn't say I'm talking behind your back. I'm just telling a story about you."

"Well, I don't appreciate you spreading rumors about me. I do *not* have superpowers. And I'm *not* paranoid!" William screamed.

"I did not scream!"

"Yes, you did."

William said, "If you don't stop talking about me, I'm going to sue you for slander!"

(Oh boy, that's my cue to skip to the next chapter.)

CHAPTER 27
Zoey

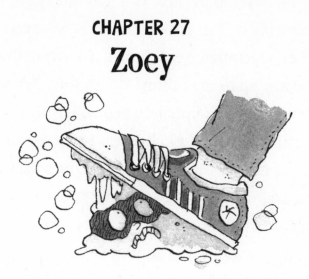

Zoey liked to be a rebel. Some days, she wore mismatched socks. *Sock rebel.* One time, she used the boys' bathroom. *Bathroom rebel.* On the day of the lightning, she even broke Ms. Linda's number one rule: NO CHEWING GUM IN CLASS. *Gum rebel.*

Unfortunately, the purple lightning struck, which put Zoey in a rather *sticky* situation....

At first, Zoey just thought her power was being pink. "I'm pink! Coolest power ever!" But when she raised her hand, it *streeeeeeeeetched* all the way up to the ceiling. When she yawned, she blew a big pink bubble. Then, when she tried to get up from her desk, her feet stuck to the floor, so she fell. As Mark walked past, he accidentally stepped on her head—and she got stuck on the bottom of his shoe.

Zoey was human gum.

"Oh crud!" Mark said. He hated stepping on gum. (Who doesn't?) He tried to peel Zoey off his shoe with a pencil.

"Ouch!" Zoey shouted. "That *hurts!*"

The more Mark and Zoey tried to separate the gum from the shoe, the more Zoey stretched.

"Who has been chewing gum in this classroom?" Ms. Linda asked, furious.

"I'm not chewing gum," Zoey said, "I *am* chewing gum."

"So are you chewing gum or aren't you?" Ms. Linda asked, confused.

"Ms. Linda, please help me!" Zoey said.

"This gum is talking!" Mason yelled, freaking out.

"A super-stretchy superpower," Fatima said, "but obviously not the best."

Together, Fatima, Ms. Linda, and Mark carefully removed Mark's shoe. They went to the school library to research how to get Zoey unstuck. According to the Internet, they could:

- Freeze her overnight in a plastic bag and then peel her off
- Pour boiling water on her
- Iron her with a clothes iron
- Use peanut butter and a knife to scrape her away

"Zoey, which would you like us to do?" Ms. Linda asked.

"None of them!" she cried. "They all sound like torture. I'd rather stay on Mark's shoe."

Mark's shoe was stuck *to* the side of Zoey's head and Zoey had one thought stuck *in* her head: Whatever happened, she would never chew gum again.

CHAPTER 28

Liam

Since the first day of class, Liam's farts had become the stuff of legend. And not because of how bad they smelled—which they did (like a tuna fish sandwich left in the sun). They were legendary because of the *amazing* things Liam could do with nothing more than the air from his butt.

Liam controlled his farts the way sculptors

sculpted clay. He could fart any pop song on demand. He could stink-bomb a target one mile away. He could fart in Morse code (which only Yuna could understand). Liam was a true f*Artist*.

To no one's surprise, the purple lightning transformed his butt blasts into something even more amazing. Liam now had SUPER-ATOMIC FARTS.

He ate a can of beans and hit the soccer field to test his new powers. "Go ahead, pull my finger," he said.

Only Teo was brave enough to do it—and only since his super-speed allowed him to pull Liam's finger and run halfway across the city to safety before

PP*BB*BBBBTTTTKA**BOOM!**

The blast left a humongous crater outside the school—and a flaming hole in Liam's underwear.

The heroes of Classroom 13 saw him as a force that could be used for good. The villains of Classroom 13 now saw him as a weapon that could be used for evil. All Liam saw was his butt hanging out in the cold air.

CHAPTER 29
Olivia

Olivia had always been the smartest person in Classroom 13. But now she was the smartest person *in the world*.

The purple lightning made her a super-genius. Her brain was so big, it popped out of her hair and glowed green anytime she had a thought. When it started glowing so bright no one could look at it, someone should have realized she had a really big idea: to take over the world.

You might think this made Olivia a super-villain, but you should ask her why first. Yes, let's ask: "Olivia, why are you going to take over the world?"

"I've done all the calculations," Olivia said. "The human race is destroying planet Earth. If we don't start fixing it now, Earth will be dead in a matter of years. Since everyone is too lazy or too greedy to fix the planet, only I can do it. But first I'll have to take over and become the world's global monarch."

See? She wants to save the planet. That's a *good reason*. But she wants to take over the world to do it. That's a *bad thing*. Sometimes, people do *bad things* for *good reasons*. It's silly but true.

Does this make Olivia a bad guy? (Or bad *girl*, in this case.) Honestly, I'm not sure. What do you think?

CHAPTER 30

Superheroes versus Super-Villains: Classroom of Justice

Olivia was going to take over the planet. But she couldn't do it alone. She needed help. So she built a Biomagnetic Antigravity Force-Field Reality Manipulator. It worked like a charm—or, more accurately, like a *magnet*—or, even more accurately, like a *superhero magnet*.

It found ~~Jay-Fu~~ Triple J ~~kung-fu~~ karate cooking at home. It found Chloe, even though she was invisible. It found Mason, even though he'd teleported to China. It even found Emma (who had been hiding under her mom's couch this whole time...silly *cat*). It found every student from Classroom 13. Then it pulled them all back.

"What are we doing in school on a *Saturday*?!" the students shouted, furious with Olivia.

Olivia explained, "The adults are destroying our planet! In a few years, there will be more plastic in the ocean than fish! Animals are becoming more endangered every day. And instead of using solar power, we're using fossil fuels, which causes pollution, which causes a greenhouse effect, which causes global warming! We have to stop them. And I know how—we have to take over the world!"

Half of the class agreed with Olivia.

The other half didn't.

"We can't take over the world," ~~Jay-Fu~~ Triple J said.

"Yes, we can, and we should!" Sophia said.

Olivia pointed to Fatima. "You're psychic. You've seen the future. What did you see?"

Fatima had to be honest. "I saw us ... *destroying the world.*"

"Then we have to save it!" Sophia said. "I'm with Olivia! Let's put all the adults in jail. Including my mom!" Half of the students cheered.

"No, wait!" said Mini-Benji. "As superheroes, we have to side with the law." Half of the students cheered.

"It looks like we have a standoff," Olivia said. "If you're not with us, you're against us. And we will have to do what all superheroes do...."

"Star in movies?" Ava asked.

"Wear tights?" Mason added.

"No!" Olivia said. "We'll have to have a super-battle!"

The kids looked at one another. No one wanted to fight, but no one wanted to destroy the planet, either.

"Let's do this!" Liam shouted. He fart-blasted the other side.

Suddenly, a super-battle broke out in the middle of Classroom 13. Mark flung corn chips at Spider-Dev the boy-spider, who shot back with webs. ~~Jay Fu~~ Triple J used his super ~~kung fu~~ karate kick on Ethan's giant robot. Teo used his super-speed to tape Preeya's mouth closed before she could sonic-scream. Hugo stepped in gum-Zoey and got stuck.

Mini-Benji saw Chloe's footprints and tied her shoelaces together so she tripped. Ximena grabbed William before he could "Bulk out!" and floated them up into the air. Emma and Isabella squared off in a battle of cat versus ~~fish~~ dolphin. They ended up in a dance-off, and everyone agreed it was a tie.

Mya & Madison couldn't decide what to wear to their first big battle, so they just kept changing outfits. They morphed into pink spike armor and blue glitter capes but couldn't choose which was cutest. They ended up missing the whole battle.

Ava used her mind-reading powers on Mason, but to no effect. (It's like he didn't even have thoughts.) Lily and Yuna were going to battle but decided it was more fun to watch. Flaming Santiago fought against Sophia, but his fire-sneezes were no match for her weather powers. Her rain put his flames out before she realized they were both on the same team. Jacob didn't have powers, but he did spray Liam's farts with air freshener.

Meanwhile, Olivia battled the super-hamster and super-cow. (Well, she didn't fight them so much as take a moment to pet the animals.)

The students were fighting and shouting so loudly that Ms. Linda heard them on the other side of town. (Of course, she did have super-hearing.) She immediately flew out of her house, across town, and into Classroom 13.

"What in the name of education are you kids doing?!" she shouted.

All the kids stopped fighting. Trying to hide behind Ms. Linda's desk, Hugo knocked over the classroom globe. It broke into several pieces.

"*Rompí el mundo*," Hugo said in Spanish. "*Lo siento.*"

Ms. Linda shook her head. "I am very disappointed in all of you. With great power comes responsibility—and all of you used your powers to make a mess."

"Wait," Fatima said. "This is good. This is great! My vision came true, but we're safe. We didn't destroy the world. We only destroyed a globe!"

"Yes, but you destroyed my favorite globe," Ms. Linda said. "You all have detention—for a week!"

✳   ✳   ✳

Later that day, the not-so-superheroes and not-evil-enough super-villains of Classroom 13 sat in detention. Ms. Linda had them writing (over and over) the following phrase:

I will _not_ destroy the world.
I will _not_ destroy the world.
I will _not_ destroy the world.

Ms. Linda noticed a strange storm cloud had appeared in the sky. The cloud was black and red, and crackled with purple electricity. It looked very familiar, but the super-teacher couldn't quite place it—at least not until it was too late.

KRAK-KA-BOOOOOOOOM!

A huge bolt of lightning crashed through the window and struck everyone in detention. Don't worry. No one was hurt. All the purple lightning did was knock out all the lights. And make every-one's hair stand straight up. Oh, and everyone lost their superpowers.

The students (and teacher) of Classroom 13 returned to their not-so-secret identities. Some would miss the excitement of superpowered life. But deep down, they all knew that in a place as unlucky as Classroom 13, every day was sort of super.

CHAPTER 31
Your Chapter

Grab some paper and a writing utensil. (Not a banana, silly. Try a pencil or pen.) Or if you have one of those fancy computer doohickeys, use that. Now, tell me...

If *YOU* could have a superpower, what would *it be*?!

When you're done writing your chapter, share it with your teacher and your family, and, of course, your friends. (Don't forget your pets. Pets like to hear stories, too, you know.)

And if you're feeling particularly adventurous, send your story to the author. He'll get a kick out of them. (No, really, I'll give him a kick. Honestly. Wait... *I'm* the author, so I *would* have to kick *myself*. Never mind. No kicks. But send me your stories.)

HONEST LEE
LITTLE, BROWN BOOKS FOR YOUNG READERS
1290 Avenue of the Americas
New York, NY 10104

Don't Miss Book 5!

Available soon!